Walt Disney Productions

presents

Henny Penny
and the Big, Bad Wolf

Random House  New York

First American Edition

Copyright © 1978 by Walt Disney Productions. All rights reserved under International and Pan-American Copyright Conventions. Published in the United States by Random House, Inc., New York, and simultaneously in Canada by Random House of Canada Limited, Toronto. Originally published in Denmark as Honsine og himlen der faldt ned by Gutenberghus Bladene, Copenhagen. ISBN: 0-394-84008-9   ISBN: 0-394-94008-3 (lib. binding).

Manufactured in the United States of America
      D   E F G H I J K   1 2 3 4

One day Henny Penny was taking a walk
in the farmyard.
All of a sudden something fell on her head—
PLONK!

"Oh, my goodness!" screeched Henny Penny.
"The sky is falling down. I must go tell
the king at once."

She ran out of the farmyard as fast as she
could go.

She was running so fast that she didn't see
her friend Mickey Mouse.

Mickey was carrying a bucket of water.

CRASH!

Up went the bucket.

Down went Mickey.

The water spilled

all over him . . .

and the bucket landed on his head!

"Quick! Get up! There is no time to waste,"
said Henny Penny. "The sky is falling down
and we must go tell the king."

Up the hill they ran, huffing and puffing.
There they saw Donald Duck, chopping logs
with his ax.

Just then a bird flew by.

The ax slipped and one of the logs hit
Donald right on the foot.

"Ouch!" squawked Donald.

He grabbed his foot
and started hopping up and down.

"Aren't you going to help me?" Donald asked.

"We have no time to waste," clucked Henny
Penny. "The sky is falling down and we must
go tell the king."

Henny Penny quickly wrapped a bandage around Donald's foot. Then she and Mickey set off again.

Donald followed along behind, muttering and
limping as he tried to keep up with his friends.

As they crossed the bridge, they saw Goofy.
He was sitting on a log, dangling his fishing
line into the stream.

But Goofy wasn't really fishing.
He was fast asleep.
And down below, the fish were swimming
around his fishing line.

Suddenly a big fish pulled on Goofy's line.
Goofy woke with a start and tumbled
head over heels into the water.

"Oh, my goodness!" said Henny Penny.
"Just look at that!"

Poor Goofy! He was up to his neck in water.

"Glub-glub," he said. "Has anyone seen that fish?"

Mickey grabbed Goofy by the collar and pulled him out of the water.

"I think you lost your fish," he said.

"Come, now! We haven't a minute to waste,"
said Henny Penny. "The sky is falling down and
we are on our way to tell the king."

"The sky is falling down? Oh, my!" said Goofy.
"I had better come with you."

So they all set off again.

At the top of the hill they came to a field.
There they found the three little pigs dancing
around with their fiddle and their flute.

"Stop that dancing right away!" shouted Henny
Penny. "Don't you know the sky is falling down?
We are on our way to tell the king."

Suddenly a voice boomed out—
"WHAT'S GOING ON HERE?"
It was the big, bad wolf!

The little group of friends huddled together.
They were afraid of the wolf.
"Mister Wolf, the sky is falling down,"
said Henny Penny very softly.

"We are on our way to tell the king."

"Well, now," said the wolf, "I just happen to know a shortcut to the king's castle. Why not follow me?"

So Henny Penny and her friends followed
the wolf out of the field and down the hill
toward the stream.

But the third little pig—the smart one—
stayed behind.

He did not trust the wolf.

Instead, the third little pig sneaked through
the tall grass to take a look at the wolf's house.

Outside in the yard a big kettle was bubbling
over a hot fire.

"That's the wolf's stew pot!" said the pig.
"If my friends aren't careful, he will pop
them right into the stew."

By this time the wolf had led everyone to
the edge of the stream.

"I am going to take you across on my raft,"
he told them.

And he leaped aboard
in one big jump.

"Come on, Miss Henny Penny," said the wolf
with a toothy smile. "Just take hold of my hand."

"Oh, my," said Henny Penny. "That *is* a big jump.
I'm not sure I can do it."

Just then the third little pig
came running up.

He whispered something
to the other two pigs.

Then one of those little pigs
whispered something to Goofy.

Goofy whispered
to Donald.

Donald whispered
to Mickey.

And Mickey whispered to Henny Penny.

"Oh, my!" said Henny Penny.
And she whispered something
to Mickey.
Mickey smiled.

"You big, bad wolf!" shouted Henny Penny.
"This isn't a shortcut at all. You are going
to take us home and cook us!"

"Me?. . .Take you home and cook you,"
said the wolf. "Whatever for?"

He did not see Mickey untying the rope that
held the raft.

Suddenly Henny Penny shouted,
"One, two, three, push!"
Everybody pushed at the raft with a stick.
The wolf was so surprised that he started
to fall over backward.

"Help me!"
he shouted.

But nobody could help the wolf.

The stream carried the raft swiftly toward a waterfall. Down it crashed.

The wolf went over, too, head first, shouting:

"H
 E
  L
   P!"

"Come on," said Mickey, pulling Henny Penny
along behind him. "Let's go home. I don't think
that the sky is going to fall down after all."

And the friends all ran home as fast as they
could go.

As for the king, nobody ever did tell him
that the sky was falling down.